CHILDREN'S
ROOM

E KATS
Hansel & Gretel :

35000097764293

CHILDREN'S ROOM

Hansel & Gretel

A Fairy Tale with a Down Syndrome Twist

by Jewel Kats

Illustrated by Claudia Marie Lenart

Loving Healing Press

Copyright © 2014 by Jewel Kats. All Rights Reserved
Illustrated by Claudia Marie Lenart
Photographed by Kristine Fiskum

Book #5 in the Fairy Ability Tales Series

Learn more about Jewel Kats at www.JewelKats.com

Library of Congress Cataloging-in-Publication Data

Kats, Jewel, 1978-
Hansel and Gretel : a fairy tale with a Down syndrome twist / by Jewel Kats ; illustrated by Claudia Lenart.
pages cm. -- (Fairy ability tales ; book 5)
Summary: "In this retelling of the classic Brothers Grimm tale, five-year-old Hansel, who has Down syndrome, is in search of food for his family. His compassion upon completing the quest frees the witch from a curse and teaches the value of forgiveness"-- Provided by publisher.
ISBN 978-1-61599-250-8 (pbk. : alk. paper) -- ISBN 978-1-61599-251-5 (hardcover : alk. paper) --
ISBN 978-1-61599-252-2 (ebook)
[1. Down syndrome--Fiction. 2. People with mental disabilities--Fiction. 3. Witches--Fiction. 4. Forgiveness--Fiction.] I. Lenart, Claudia, 1958- illustrator. II. Title.
PZ7.K157445Han 2014
[E]--dc23
2014033027

Distributed by Ingram (USA/CAN/AU), Bertram's Books (UK/EU)

Loving Healing Press
5145 Pontiac Trail
Ann Arbor, MI 48105

Toll free (USA/CAN) 888-761-6268
www.LHPress.com
info@LHPress.com

The Fairy Ability Tales

Cinderella's Magical Wheelchair:
An Empowering Fairy Tale

The Princess and the Ruby:
An Autism Fairy Tale

Snow White's Seven Patches:
A Vitiligo Fairy Tale

The Princess Panda Tea Party:
A Cerebral Palsy Fairy Tale

Hansel & Gretel:
A Fairy Tale with a Down Syndrome Twist

Also by Jewel Kats:

DitzAbled Princess:
A Comical Diary Inspired by Real Life

Miss Popular Steals the Show:
Girls in Wheelchairs Rule!

Teddy Bear Princess:
A Story About Sharing and Caring

Reena's Bollywood Dream:
A Story about Sexual Abuse

What Do You Use To Help Your Body?
Maggie Explores the World of Disabilities

Word Search Divas

One fateful night, a storm ripped through Cottage Country. People—small and large—hid in their basements. Strong, long trees hit the ground under loud claps of thunder. Nothing but lightning bolted through darkness. Fear hung in the air of this once rainbow-kissed secret place.

The rain finally stopped pouring days and days later. Cottage Country was deserted. The only people left were a fisherman and his family.

They had managed all this time with a hidden supply of food. However, now their cupboards were empty. Hunger had crept into their bellies.

"What will I feed our two children?" his wife asked in a quiet, shaking voice.

The fisherman grabbed a large burlap sack. "You needn't worry. I know just what to do," he said and proceeded to call for their children.

Hansel and Gretel soon appeared. Their clothes were terribly worn and torn. Hansel's stomach let out a grumble. Their mother looked down with what appeared to be shame. The fisherman took the burlap sack and went up to his daughter.

"Give me your hand," the fisherman said.

The young girl—no more than nine—opened her calloused palm.

The fisherman placed the sack in her hands. "The future of this family lies with you. I want you to take this sack and go out to the forest and find whatever food you can. Return only when the bag is full."

Hansel twisted his foot. "Can I help?" he asked.

Their mother gasped. She leapt to her feet. She caressed her son's face.

"You're sick, Hansel," his mother began to cry. "You won't be able to help in the least—especially at just five years old."

The fisherman interjected. "You've always been too overprotective of the boy. He's not sick. He has Down syndrome. Let him go out in the world. At the very least, he can keep his sister company."

The children listened to their father and off they went. Both Hansel and Gretel could hear their mother crying as they left. Gretel's heart flip-flopped. So did Hansel's.

"I don't even know where this forest is…" Gretel grumbled under the massive weight her father had placed on her shoulders.

"That's easy! Follow me," Hansel said. "I used to play under the bushes all the time. Remember how I caught poison ivy there?"

His sister nodded. "Yes, I remember. That's why I was never allowed even to look in that direction. Mamma spent so many weeks tending to your itchy wounds."

Hansel giggled. "She sure did. Mamma gave me lots of kisses, too."

Hansel took the lead. Gretel followed after him. She was huffing, puffing, and losing her breath.

"Would you slow down, Hansel?!" Gretel said with annoyance.

There were heaps of tree branches on the ground everywhere. She had to jump over one after the next.

Hansel got a mischievous twinkle in his eyes. "Now that Mamma and Papa aren't here, I can do as I please. Nobody is the boss of me."

Gretel brushed hair off her face. "This isn't about who rules the roost. We're here to collect food."

Hansel kicked a pile of pebbles. "I don't see why we can't have a little fun?"

Right then, Hansel took off. He was running at the speed of a soaring kite.

Now, Hansel had the ability to run super quick. Even though he fell along the way, he'd get up with a heartfelt laugh.

Dirty soil was splattered all over his cheeks. His pants bore even bigger holes now. Hansel didn't have a care in the world.

His sister, Gretel, grew more and more worried as her brother ran deeper into the forest. She tried to keep up, but she was soon losing sight of him.

She fell to the ground with tears spilling in every direction. Her burlap sack had nothing in it. Her brother had scampered off to goodness knows where.

"What will I ever tell Mamma and Papa?" Gretel screamed into the mucky forest.

Not one person heard her.

Meanwhile, Hansel was enjoying his new freedom. He had no one to answer to—except for his belly that kept grumbling and rumbling. He knew he was somewhere deep in the forest. He was growing more tired and thirsty. Soon enough, a peculiar cottage caught his eye in the distance. He decided to run towards it.

When he finally arrived, Hansel couldn't believe what he saw. Never even in his wildest dreams had he ever seen anything like it—for it was a real-life house made entirely of candy! The bricks were created from chocolate. Candy canes sprouted from the ground. Sugar icing was spread above on the rooftop. The windows were made of cinnamon sticks. Hansel's small hands didn't know in which direction to head. He thrust his fist forward and grabbed off decorative marshmallows that he swallowed quick, quick, quick! Everything he ate just grew right back. It was pure magic at its finest.

As Hansel feasted, he thought of his sister, Gretel, and her burlap sack. If only she were here, they could take candy back for their family.

"Well, well, well, look at who's arrived at our door step...." An ill-sounding voice interrupted Hansel's gobbling merriment.

Hansel looked up to see a witch clad in black with a green toad on her shoulder. She even had a broomstick perched by her side.

Hansel gasped.

"It's one of those people with Down syndrome," the talking toad said.

"Yes! Our very first guest with a disability!" the witch cackled.

The young boy quickly brushed crumbs off his face. "I have a name," he said with bravado. "My name is Hansel."

"He talks, too!" the toad went on. It was as if Hansel were not present. "I'm sure he'll make for a fine supper."

"I agree. I just wonder how stupid this kid with Down syndrome is?!" the witch stated.

Hansel ran up to the witch. He kicked her in the shin. The witch lost her balance and fell over flat, also knocking down the toad and the boy.

Hansel jumped to his feet. "I'm smart enough to do this!" He'd grabbed her broomstick. "You can't fly without this, can you?" he mocked this time.

The toad and the witch looked on with horror.

"Give that back to me at once!" the witch demanded.

"I'll give it back because it belongs to you, but I won't be doing it so fast..." Hansel said.

"What do you want?" the toad asked.

"I want you to take me inside your home, and give me the secret ingredients and potion to create a Candy House for my family," Hansel said while holding onto the magical broomstick extra tight.

The toad let out a horrible, painful squeal. "We can't do that! It took years and years to perfect the recipe to create a Candy House."

The witch sighed. "What choice do we have?" she said quietly. "Without that broom I can't fly, and we'll both shrink into tiny ice sculptures at the next full moon. My family's been in this business for years. I didn't make up the rules."

Hansel smiled. "It looks like we have a deal?"

The toad and witch said nothing and started heading inside their home. Hansel followed.

The Candy House was a sweet-tooth lover's dream. Candy, candy, and more candy was stuffed inside. There was also a large book titled *The Magic Book of Spells*. Behind it were potions and all sorts of smelly ingredients.

The witch grabbed a bottle. She shoved it into Hansel's pocket. "Here you go..." she said with a tear in her eye.

For some reason, Hansel felt pity for the old woman. "Tell you what," he said. "Why don't we all go to my family's home? You can create the forever Candy House for us. Then, I'd like you and Toad to be the first guests to join us for dinner."

"Really?" the toad and witch said together.

"Nobody's ever done that for me before..." the witch said quietly.

"Lots of things happen for the first time," Hansel answered.

The toad, witch and Hansel hopped onto the broomstick. They flew to Hansel's family's cottage. Gretel had returned home safely.

Mamma and Papa were awestruck when, with the sprinkle of some potion on worn grass, their very own Candy House sprouted up. The family sat down to have dinner for the first time in many, many days. Everyone was hungry.

The fisherman looked at his son, Hansel, the witch, and the toad. "I will be forever grateful to you all."

Hansel peered at the witch and the toad. "I would like to give you the first of our food as our special guests," he said, handing them a basket of cookies.

The witch was so touched by this act of kindness that she began to cry tears of joy. As this happened, she miraculously turned into a beautiful maiden. The toad became a tiny puppy. The whole family was shocked.

"What should we call you?" Hansel asked the young blonde woman before him.

"Mirella," she answered. "My name has always been Mirella, but people just called me 'The Witch.'"

The young boy stuck out his hand. "I can relate. My name has always been Hansel."

"Hansel is much more than Down syndrome," his mother piped in.

"He's my brother," Gretel said.

"He's my son," Papa said.

"Hansel is my friend," Mirella said.

The puppy barked.

And so, their family's new friendship began...

THE END

About the Author

Once a teen runaway, Jewel Kats is now a two-time Mom's Choice Award winner and Gelett Burgess gold medalist. For six years, Jewel penned a syndicated teen advice column for Scripps Howard News Service (USA) and *The Halifax Chronicle Herald*. She gained this position through The Young People's Press.

Her books have been featured in *Ability Magazine* (USA) twice. She's authored nine books—six are about disabilities. **The Museum of disABILITY History** celebrated her work with a two-day event. Jewel has appeared as an international magazine cover story four times! Recently, her work was featured in an in-depth article published in *The Toronto Star*. Jewel's work has also appeared as an evening news segment on WKBW-TV and on the pages of *The Buffalo News* and *The Huffington Post*.

Please visit her online at www.jewelkats.com

About the Illustrator

Claudia Marie Lenart is a fiber artist from northern Illinois. She experimented in the arts and handwork since childhood and while pursuing a career as a journalist. She finally found her true muse when she discovered needle felting.

Her soft sculpture characters are created by repeatedly poking wool and other natural fibers, like alpaca, with a barbed needle.

Claudia also uses a variety of other techniques to create her wool illustrations including wet felting and pressed wool painting. To see her work visit www.claudiamariefelt.com

Hansel & Gretel and other great books on Down syndrome can be found at every GiGi's Playhouse Down Syndrome Achievement Centers location across the US and Mexico.

GiGi's Playhouse makes a lifetime commitment to participants and their families, and each location provides unique educational and therapeutic programs in a format that individuals with Down syndrome learn best. All programs aim to maximize acceptance and self-confidence, and intend to empower children and adults to achieve their greatest potential. All educational, therapeutic and career training programs are offered to families at no charge.

Down Syndrome Achievement Centers
educate. inspire. believe.

confident u • healthy u • whole u

HANDMADE • HEARTFELT • HOPE FILLED

www.GiGisPlayhouse.org

Cinderella's Magical Wheelchair: An Empowering Fairytale

Join Cinderella in a World Where Anything is Possible!
In a Kingdom far, far away lives Cinderella. As expected, she slaves away for her cranky sisters and step-mother. She would dearly love to attend the Royal costume ball and meet the Prince, but her family is totally dead set against it. In fact, they have gone so far as to trash her wheelchair! An unexpected magical endowment to her wheelchair begins a truly enchanted evening and a dance with the Prince. Can true love be far behind?

- This fairy tale demonstrates people with disabilities can overcome abuse
- Children with disabilities finally have a Cinderella story they can identify with
- In this version, Cinderella uses her own abilities to build a new future for herself
- The connection Cinderella and the Prince share illustrates love surges past mutual attraction

"An inspiring and exciting read for children of all ages and abilities. Finally here is a book which shows that wheelchair-mobile children can achieve anything. A clever, modern twist on this traditional and much loved story."
--Joanne Smith, TV Producer, *Terry Fox Hall of Fame inductee, Gemini Award winner*

Book #1 in the Fairy Abilities Tales Series from Loving Healing Press
Cinderalla's Magical Wheelchair: An Empowering Fairytale
ISBN 978-1-61599-112-9
Available at Amazon.com, Barnes & Noble, and other children's book retailers

The Princess and the Ruby: An Autism Fairy Tale

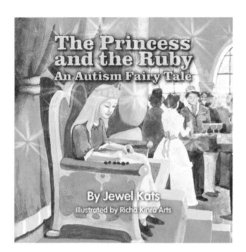

A Mysterious Girl Puts the Future of a Kingdom in the Balance!

One icy-cold winter night, everything changes: a young girl shows up at the king and new queen's castle doorstep wearing little more than a purple jacket and carrying a black pouch. The king recognizes the mystery girl's identity as the long-lost princess without her uttering even a single word. However, the new queen refuses to believe the king's claims. In turn, a devious plan is hatched... and, the results are quite fitting!

- This new twist on Hans Christen Andersen's *The Princess and the Pea* is surely to be loved by all fairy tale enthusiasts.
- *The Princess and the Ruby: An Autism Fairy Tale* adds to much-needed age-appropriate literature for girls with Autism Spectrum Disorder.
- Both fun and education are cleverly weaved in this magical tale, teaching children to be comfortable in their own skin and to respect the differences of others.

"The Princess and the Ruby is a heartwarming narrative; a tale that beautifully depicts several unique characterizations of Autism Spectrum Disorder. Jewel Kats has refreshingly shed light upon a daily struggle to redefine 'normalized behaviors', in an admirable effort to gain societal acceptance and respect."

--Vanessa De Castro, Primary Residential Counselor with Autistic Youth

Book #2 in the Fairy Abilities Tales Series from Loving Healing Press
The Princess and the Ruby: An Autism Fairy Tale
ISBN 978-1-61599-175-4
Available at Amazon.com, Barnes & Noble, and other children's book retailers

Snow White's Seven Patches: A Vitiligo Fairy Tale

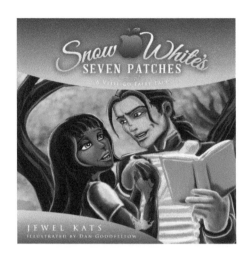

Snow White's Seven Patches: A Vitiligo Fairy Tale is a modern-day story with the classical theme of good conquering evil. You'll find the age-old ingredients of a magic mirror, poisonous apple, dwarfs, and romance here. However, this adaptation includes a vain mother who's so clouded by beauty myths that she keeps her own daughter a secret, while plagiarizing the workings of her mind. Everything falls apart when the good mirror finally speaks the truth.

Young readers with vitiligo will look at their own skin patches with a unique lens, finding interesting shapes and stories behind each puffy cloud of white.

- Readers will be introduced to the firsthand-hurt that plagiarism can cause through Snow White's experience.
- The loving dwarf family illustrates that helping people in need should be a priority in life.
- Readers learn that not all princesses look alike.
- The concept of "beauty is within the eye of the beholder" is exemplified by the prince and magic mirror.

"In *Snow White's Seven Patches*, Jewel emphasizes how to overcome adversity with creativity. She encourages children to maintain a healthy perspective about their physical appearance. Jewel reminds us that despite wickedness, we can move on and get about the business of life."
--Carole Di Tosti, novelist, reviewer for Blogcritics.com

Book #3 in the Fairy Abilities Tales Series from Loving Healing Press
Snow White's Seven Patches: A Vitiligo Fairy Tale
ISBN 978-1-61599-206-5
Available at Amazon.com, Barnes & Noble, and other children's book retailers

CPSIA information can be obtained
at www.ICGtesting.com
Printed in the USA
BVHW020757260919
559194BV00004B/9/P